SHUTAO LIAO

MEDITATION AT THE FOOT OF THE HIMALAYAS

Copyright © 2024 by Shutao Liao

All rights reserved. No part of this publication may be reproduced, stored or transmitted in any form or by any means, electronic, mechanical, photocopying, recording, scanning, or otherwise without written permission from the publisher. It is illegal to copy this book, post it to a website, or distribute it by any other means without permission.

Second edition

This book was professionally typeset on Reedsy. Find out more at reedsy.com

Contents

MEDITATION AT THE FOOT OF THE HIMALAYAS	1
Preface	4
1	6
2	9
3	12
4	16
5	18
6	22
7	24
8	26
9	28
10	29
11	31
12	33
13	35
14	36
15	37
16	38
17	39
18	41
19	42
20	44
21	45
22	47

23	48
24	50
25	51
26	52
27	55
28	56
29	57
On the Spirituality of the 21st Century Poetry	58
POSTSCRIPT	67
About the Author	69

MEDITATION AT THE FOOT OF THE HIMALAYAS

Shutao Liao

MEDITATION AT THE FOOT OF THE HIMALAYAS

The Author

MEDITATION AT THE FOOT OF THE HIMALAYAS

DEDICATED TO FREE, UNYIELDING, BEAUTIFUL SOULS

Preface

The writing process of this epic poem satisfied my desire for grand poetry. It is a courageous challenge to the boundaries of imagination and spirit. Like a sailor sailing in the sea, I have no way to retreat but to move forward to the unknown shore.

In the past few years, I have picked up the pen to write this epic poem several times, had to put it down in disappointment and then forgot about it. I have to thank a magical night, many beautiful poetry lines crowded into my dreams until I woke up. The epic of dozens of pages long, had already completed its prototype at that moment.

Therefore, only half of this collection of the epic poem was written by me using my own brainpower. Some of the images and sentences were automatically formed in dreams. It is the result of the perfect combination of unconsciousness, subconsciousness and consciousness. The sentences formed

Preface

unconsciously in my sleep continued to flow out in disorder in my subconscious mind. Later, in my consciousness, I struggled to build them into palace-like lines of poetry. Like an insatiable chef, I wandered between thousands of seasonings, colors, and flavors before making my final choice. My thoughts and imagination revolved around the subject, describing it from different angles and levels, in order to achieve a broad and profound effect.

In this increasingly chaotic and corrupt world, how much I miss those days of beautiful literature and hungry readers. I wholeheartedly want to add a touch of literary beauty to this era, and I hope that the publication of this epic poem can fulfill my wish.

1

This is Bagada in Nepal,
  Bighi River sleeps at the foot of the Himalayas,
  Melting snow from glaciers,
Ceaselessly infuses this eternal flow.

Firm
  Rocks,
  Soft and airy
  Red earth,
  Vegetation covered by pine forests,
  Sleeping veins,
  Decay, life, death,
  But countless stories have been forgotten,
  There is also hope, suffering, unspeakable sorrow, and helpless fate.

In the soft wetlands, in the soil, in the glaciers, under the mineral veins,

1

Rapid changes,
Life always came unexpectedly,
And left in a suddenness,

No goodbyes were said, no traces of their existence were left behind.

It's here,
  Time
  Squeezed slowly
  Until solidified
  By silence,
  Like a dead person who has been buried long ago,
  A forgotten past,
  It has long since lost its smell of decay,
  Only hydrated ice works continuously
  Washing the river bed,
  Whispering with those silent fish and water creatures,

Along the mountains,
  Along the villages where smoke rises,
  Along the roots of the ravines,
  Draws out those metaphorical shapes that no one knows,
  Like a dream, like an illusion, like life or death.

The earth here is the face of an ancient wise man,
  Through countless centuries,
  Constructed with ravines and suffering,
  Wind, rain and frost,
  Beaten, tortured, ravaged,
  Endures for the sake of existence,

MEDITATION AT THE FOOT OF THE HIMALAYAS

Like Prometheus,
Scars are everywhere, and tears are intertwined.

2

The majestic Himalayas cover the sky and the sun,
Insert heavily into the heart of the earth,
Will
Makes them tower into the clouds-filled sky,
On the top of the world,
Their every slight breath shakes the earth,
Transforms into tsunamis, landslides, violent storms,
Even the hellfire rushing inside the rock formations
Is also pressed into the deep ocean.

Huge body
Buried countless ancient legends.

God's hands
In the process of existence
Cut the elements of the soul:

Greed, lust, hatred, envy, desire, courage, honor, kindness and

MEDITATION AT THE FOOT OF THE HIMALAYAS

love,
>Shown one by one in the history of nature.

Even so,
>How could I
>In the thousands of tears that surged through history
>To tell which ones are fake? What are the intoxicating touches? What are the heart-shaking pains?

Ah free souls that escape from the shackles of thoughts,
>May you enjoy wandering in these vast ice peaks,
>Above sea level
>At a height of nine thousand meters,

Everest
>K2
>Kanchenjunga
>Lhotse
>Makalu
>Cho Oyu
>Dhaulagiri
>Manaslu
>Nanga Parbat
>Annapurna
>Gasherbrum I
>Broad Peak
>Shisha Pangma and Gasherbrum II.

Those fearless climbers,
>Carrying courage wrapped in death,
>Come here again and again,

2

Falling time after time,
Sliding towards the endless valley of ice.

3

Hugo est entré dans mon rêve,
    Me parlant de ses "Les Misérables" et des trois chaînes majeures de la vie,
J'ai répondu:
"Arrêtez, monsieur !
J'ai moi-même vu trop de souffrance !" [1]

I,
    An escapee from the "civilized world",
    A wanderer covered with scars,
    A hopeless sleepwalker,

Came here in September,
    Now sit on a wooden bench in front of the gravel house.

This is a strong autumn,
    The wind is bleak,
    The scattered leaves swirl in the rolling atmosphere,

3

I hold my breath and listen to the harmonial sound of the universe
   Trying to parse its hidden meaning,
   The mud reflects the golden afterglow of the sunset,
   The tides of the soul have drowned my thoughts,
   What a desolate and beautiful plight!

I can't help but recite Li Sao's desperate poem,
   With unchanging pride, [2]

Thinking about the past and present,
   Just like Dante who was on the run,
   Fleeing in the dark nights, not knowing where he was,
   And didn't know where he would end up in the future.

I bend down
   In the echoes of the air
   Pick up those dry leaves that died long ago,
   Feeling sad for their lost lives,
   They should be standing on the branches at this moment,
   But withered in the season of youth,

Just like those descendants of the northern kingdom,
   It hasn't been long since they bloomed,
   Soon withered and died.

You lonely traveler
   Unable to bear the weight of life,
   Hold on for love,
   Happy with thoughts,
   In this journey through the wilderness of the world,

MEDITATION AT THE FOOT OF THE HIMALAYAS

    Carrying that desperate escape,
    Come here.

I may be nostalgic for these vast ice peaks,
    Watch the sunshine on the boundless forests,
    Look at the stars all over the deep night sky,
    Feel the embrace of all things in the flow of time.

Ah spirit of all things in the Himalayas, the eternal Lord,
    Let me tell you,
    I am a recluse
    Have made up my mind,
    With my humble hands and faith in my life,
    In this corner of the world,
    Rebuild a palace of fraternity,
    And pray daily surrounded by its mercy;
    I want to use pure thoughts
    Wash away the dust of the world;
    I want to curl my limbs,
    In their kind touch
    Stay away from all the ugliness and evil in the world.

I want to thank my father, mother, relatives, and friends;
    Thank every stranger's face met by chance, every different landscape, every natural breath;
    Thank for the coming of spring, summer, autumn and winter;
    Thank the clouds, thank the wind, thank the rain, thank the thunder, thank the lightning, thank the storm.

I also want to thank for all the sufferings in my life,
    Without their deep embraces again and again,

3

How could I be so close to the truth of life?

How is it possible to understand the exciting splendor of the human world?

Without their deep embraces again and again,

How can I understand

What is ugliness? What is despicable? What is fraud? What is the pain of life, separation and death? What is beauty?

And what is the true meaning of love?

[1]

In French, English translation is:

Hugo entered my dream,
 Telling me about his "The Miserable Ones" and the three major shackles of life,
 I replied:
 "Stop it, sir!
 I have seen too much suffering myself!"

The three major shackles of life are: religion, society and nature.

[2]

"Li Sao" was a famous epic poem written by Chinese ancient poet Qu Yuan on his exile at the Warring States period, Li means departure, Sao is a writing style.

4

I saw the strong oak tree growing,
    Standing straight in the storm,
    In the passage of centuries
Has it witnessed how many lives and deaths? How much hope and disillusionment? How many joys and sorrows?

Withered fallen cherry blossoms are scattered in the wind and dust,
    They were once strong, once bright and full of youth,
    But can only die in the mud,
    Forgotten by people, trampled by passers-by,
    Who can remember their beauty?
    And care about their fate?

The wind from the valley
    Passing through the vegetation, passing the stone stairs, passing the sheep and cattle, passing the houses, giving me many salty kisses,

4

    Bringing the scent of glaciers and ocean,
    Its casual access
    There is sadness and melancholy, but also the desire for spring, as well as longing and dreams for relatives far away.

Mountain peaks sometimes disappear into the atmosphere,
    Like a reclusive hermit who has lost his whereabouts,
    When the sun sets on the distant mountain ridges,
    The fleeing stars reappear in the silent firmament.

The sound of the ocean tides echoes across the horizon,
    In those silent nights,
    Those innocent nights,
    Those nights without sadness,
    Those nights filled with the scent of larch,
    Those nights that smell of moist strawberries,
    Those nights unforgettable because of lover's kisses,
    Those nights guarded by sheepdogs,
    Those nights ravaged by the torture of time,
    And those nights that are soft because of love.

5

The owner of the stone house
    A strong Sherpa woman,
    With bronzed skin,
It is a masterpiece of clouds, rain, wind, frost and sunshine,
Her smile is solemn with sufferings,
Showing the harsh life,
Already integrated with the spirits here,
Bushes, stones, streams, mountain breeze.

Every night, she would kneel in front of her home and pray devoutly,
    Put her hands on her chest, then raise them high above the head, and then push down heavily on the ground.
    Say prayers thousands of times,
        Listen to the various strange sounds coming from the valley,
        Feel the breaths of nature,
        Talk to the elves,
        In the drowsy and hazy dreams.

5

"I love you, no matter who you are, I just need to know that you are a human being, or a life is enough!" She said.

Whether you are an Asian, Arab, European, African or American,
   Wherever you come from,
   What kind of faith you have.

We are all prisoners chased by fate,
   From the time we were born, shackled on the body and the mind,
   Already submerged in the tides of mortal desires,
   And what we really need
   love and tolerance
   But never really owned them.

Even if time exerts all its tortures,
   Nor can we lose the beauty of life,
   Please bring kindness, tolerance and fraternity,
   Embarrass them tightly,
   After experiencing the ups and downs of the human world,
   You can still have a pure heart,
   What a magnificent and unyielding broad mind!

Life is just a fleeting phenomenon,
   Like dewdrops in the morning light, like a wisp of smoke,
   Even though we know this, we are still too focused on it,
   Mistaking it for an eternal abode,
   Working hard for it, being evil for it, hurting selves's body for it that could be at ease,
   Only the wise have already regarded it as an illusion,

MEDITATION AT THE FOOT OF THE HIMALAYAS

Take the sufferings of this life
As Noah's Ark of nirvana to another world.

Those emperors and generals
   In the end, they were just dry bones in the tombs, deserted in the wind and rain.

No matter what, death will visit on time,
   All tricks are just futile games after all,
   The air melts into the air,
   Dust disappears into dust.

Please put down the burden of your life,
   Ideological obsession,
   The dust in life,
   Worldly troubles,
   Desires that make people unable to control themselves,
   Here and now at this place
   To become a complete person,
   Sitting by this cozy fire basin,
   Let me pass you a cup of thick milk tea,
   Forget about the sufferings and sadness of life for a moment.

Silvery white snowflakes are flying all over the sky,
   Covered the roads,
   Covered the wilderness,
   Covered the houses,
   Covered the forests,
   Flickering lights from farmhouses windows
   Like stars dotting the blurry night sky,
   All living things are hiding in their lairs

5

Listen to the fleeting sound of the wind.

Destiny,
  As unstable as the climate here,
  It should be noted that in nature,
  We are just passers-by,
  The same as such snow falling in the wind,
  Like a phantom that cannot be saved,
  Nothing can be taken when leaving,
  Destined to return to dust.

We are descendants of Sherpa, Gurung, Rai, Lepcha, Khas, Dogras, Khasas, Kirati, Tamang, Limbu, Bhotiya, Newar, Sunuwar, Chhetri, Yolmo, Sarki, Walung and Pahari,
  Living in this corner of the Himalayas for generations,
  Looking up at heights that make even the most skilled eagles feel timid,
  Worshiping this sacred palace of nature.

Buckeye, alder, poplar, birch, willow, rhododendron, laurel, chestnut, blue pine, cedar, spruce, fir, bayberry, blackberry, maple, oak, shrub; wild yak, bharal, domestic yak, tahr, wild boar, American black bear, markhor,

Reproduction, birth, growth, death,
  Endless cycle,

Take place in this faraway corner of the world.

6

Along the banks of the sacred Ganges, Yamuna and Saraswati rivers,
   On Sunday countless bathers came,
Immersing themselves in holy water,
Washing away sins:

The evil of desire,
   The evil of deception,
   The evil of greed,
   The evil of jealousy,
   The evil of hatred,
   The evil of faith.

Look at your own hands,
   How many tragedies have been caused in the world?
   Look at your own souls,
   How much evil lives there?
   Look at your own footprints,

6

Why do you always walk in the devil's territory?
Your ears,
Why can't hear the voice of mercy?

Don't you know that it is a sin in this world to have more wealth than you need?
    It is a delicacy cooked with the suffering of all living beings,
    In reincarnation
    He who oppresses others will be oppressed,
    He who enslaves others will be enslaved,
    He who gives pain to others will take back that pain.

You irredeemable people
    In thousands of actions,
    Regard falsehood as truth,
    Living in fraud,
    Such a crime
    How could it be dissolved in holy water?

7

Who are we? Why must we accept the cruel arrangements of fate, the miserable situation, and the visit of death without exception?

The brave meditator asked:

"God of death, why don't you always show even a little bit of kindness to let me retain my beloved relatives and bring me the pain of separation and death?"

God of death replied:

"I am merciful,
　Let you say goodbye when it's time to say goodbye,
　Let you finish when it's time to finish,
　To die,
　It's just a dream that's been called back by time,
　The feast will always come to an end,

7

Meaningless existence is the greatest sorrow and sin in the world.
Those fallen leaves drifting down in the wind,
Will definitely fall into the soil,
Become beneficial elements again,
That is their best destination,
Because they have withered and decayed,
Only death is the ultimate salvation of lives."

8

T he holy woman said:

We Himalayan people who have lived here for generations,
So close to death,
Therefore, we must pray before three meals a day,
Meditating on death.

Dawn Meditation
    For the beginning of birth
    We have just escaped the emptiness of darkness,
    Can't remember the reason of past life,
    Haven't solved the fate of this life yet,
    Although have a pure body,
    But the reincarnation of cause and effect is already doomed;

Midday meditation
    Just like the strong sunshine,

8

The soul is drowned in the ocean of desires,
Don't know that the god of death is already waiting on the road,
Waving its destiny of Zen stick;

Night meditation
Waiting peacefully for the call of death,
Accept the cycle of life and decay,
No sorrow, no joy, no worry, no delight,
Return to the earth,
Return to the forests,
Return to the wind,
Return to the clouds,
Return to the rain,
Return to the emptiness.

9

The hermit who came here on pilgrimage,
    Carrying the soul of a wanderer,
    He likes to write in his poems
Buddhist verses or biblical metaphors
Even if he quotes them, he won't understand,
With the purpose of no purpose, the direction of no direction,
Talking to the god of wind on the top of the Himalayas.

10

I come from a remote town,
    Have been floating in the sea of desire for too long,
    Even death could not stop my desires,
Tasted the wine of desire in the sea of bitterness;

I come from continental Europe,
    Once focused on conquest,
    Planted honor in cruel soil,
    Now it has become a heavy burden;

I come from a prosperous city,
    Spent my youth there in the feast,
    I betrayed others and was betrayed by others,
    Until I could no longer bear the ugliness of the world;

I come from a village on the banks of the Ganges,
    Washed away my sorrow with holy water day after day,
    Then went back to wallowing in the world of mortals,

MEDITATION AT THE FOOT OF THE HIMALAYAS

Decades passed like that,
Now I just want to wait here quietly for death.

We are a group of people who meet by chance,
   Bringing the breath of Ghaghara River
   And the dust on the highways.

An old monk,
   Standing in the cold wind of Kailash Mountain
   Greets us.

Forget highways, computers, the Internet, artificial intelligence,
   After all, we are just tiny creatures,
   Amuse ourselves in the mortal world,
   Immerse in the fleeting emptiness.

11

The palace of heaven and the palace of earth,
    Eighteen Arhats stand on both sides,
    Only when The Six Sense Roots are pure can you cross,
    The end of cycle of West Bliss,
    The red dust is billowing in The Dream of NanKe,
    Cause and effect are shown here; [1], [2], [3]

The gate of ghosts, the palace of the king of hell,
    The king of hell turns over his fortune book to see your fate,
    Rakshasa and imp come to seduce your soul,
    There are eighteen hells for you to choose from,
    The sin is unforgivable,
    It will be repaid in every life.

[1]

MEDITATION AT THE FOOT OF THE HIMALAYAS

The Six Sense Roots in Buddhism refer to the six sense organs of the human body and their related cognitive abilities, specifically:

Eye (vision)
  Ear (hearing)
  Nose (smell)
  Base of tongue (taste)
  Sense of touch (touch)
  Meaning (consciousness)

[2]

West Bliss is the translation of the Sanskrit name Sukhâvatî. It refers to the Pure Land of Amitabha Buddha. Also known as the Pure Land of Ultimate Bliss, Land of Ultimate Bliss, Western Pure Land, West, Western Heaven, Peaceful Pure Land, Peaceful World, and Peaceful Kingdom.

[3]

Chinese idiom "The Dream of NanKe", which metaphorically refers to life as a dream, wealth and fortune are unpredictable; it also generally refers to a dream.

12

Amitabha! Amitabha! Amitabha! [1]

[1]

The meaning of Amitabha can be understood from the following aspects:

Religious significance: In Buddhism, Amitabha is considered the leader of the Western Paradise, representing infinite light and life.

Cultural expression: In daily life, Amitabha is also used as a mantra to express prayers, thanks or sighs.

Philosophical connotation: From a deeper understanding, the name Amitabha contains immeasurable wisdom and immeasurable awareness, and represents the concept of immeasurable light and *longevity.*

13

Your knowledge is your ignorance,
    Let go of desires,
    Let go of your attachments,
Put aside your prejudices,
Living in the moment,
Possess this perfection of soul and body.

14

We are a group of wizards who cast spells,
Accustomed to traveling between the human world and the underworld, the past and the future,
Everything that happens is an arrangement of fate,
Birth and death, happiness and sorrow are just two sides of a copper coin,
All the joys, sorrows and happiness of the world are here,
Let us wave the magic Zen wand,
Characters, spells plus material elements,
Between past and future
Invite those ghosts in the woods to go with,
Good destiny and bad retribution
All will be revealed in the necessity of existence.

15

The forgotten dead are resurrected in dreams,
   In the burning soul,
   Reproduce human history, religion, beliefs and cruel civilization,
  People live in desires,
  Lost direction.

16

Goshawks soar in the blue sky,
Animals curl in their caves,
Birds live in dense forests,
Each has its own end,
All have to endure the pain of reincarnation.

17

Now that we have come to this world,
    Now that the charming bonfire has been lit,
    Why not leave sadness behind,
Around the blazing flames,
Naked souls,
Let's have a round dance together.

Death is just another unforgettable journey,
    Put aside the soot and dust of Seven Emotions and Six Desires for the time being,
    In the passing of life
    Enjoy this happy moment to the fullest,
    Like life, death is just an illusion of existence,
    Beloved relatives
    Are waiting for us to go. [1]

We will reunite with them in another world,
    Share the happy time there,

MEDITATION AT THE FOOT OF THE HIMALAYAS

In a corner of heaven
Drink the nectar of everlasting life,
Everything in this mortal world is empty,
Only love can overcome all obstacles,
Keep all the touches of life.

[1]

Seven Emotions and Six Desires: refers to various human emotions and desires.

Seven Emotions: seven kinds of human emotions, generally referring to happiness, anger, sadness, fear, love, evil and desire.

Six Desires: Buddhism refers to six desires: lust, appearance, majesty and posture, words and sounds, smoothness, desire for each other, which generally refers to various human desires.

18

The snowmen hidden among the ice peaks,
Just hermits who are tired of the world!

19

When the temple bells ring,
   We sit together,
     Entering into the meditation practice of great enlightenment.

Mortal enlightenment
   Everything is empty,
   Get rid of the joys and the sorrows of the four seasons,
   To accommodate the creation of heaven and earth,
   Follow Bodhidharma, the wise man in the world. [1]

[1]

Bodhidharma, a South Indian, a Zen monk in the Northern and Southern Dynasties of China, free translation is Awakening Dharma. According to "The Biography of the Eminent Monk", the South

19

Indian belonged to the Kshatriya caste, had thorough knowledge of Mahayana Buddhism, and was a cultivator of Buddhism, respected by those who practice meditation.

20

Everything is the same,
　　All spirits are of the same nature,
　　All things have the same destiny,
They are all legends performed by metal, wood, water, fire and earth in time and space.

21

Today
    We come here,
        Put on the black gauze,
Write an elegiac couplet,
Present a wreath,
Put on white linen,
Together we mourn the loss of a life.

Now that you are dead,
    We will remember your virtues and forget your meanness,
    Miss you with pity,
    Death has wiped everything away,
    Hell and heaven will have their own retribution for your reincarnation.

In the funeral procession
    There are your father, mother, children, lovers, relatives, friends, fellow villagers, tribesmen, and even your enemies.

MEDITATION AT THE FOOT OF THE HIMALAYAS

You died on a high mountain,
   Died in the rice fields,
   Died in an unforgettable summer,
   Died on a bitterly cold winter day,
   Died in a brutal killing,
   Died in bomb smoke,
   Died in the arms of loved ones.

Let us bury you on a tree trunk in the forest
   Talk to the birds;
   Let us bury you deep by the lake
   Snuggle up with the vegetation;
   let us throw you into the sea
   Sleep with the water;
   Let us give you back to the sky
   Fly with angels.

Soil faces soil,
   Dust turns to dust,
   Air goes back to air.

You once had a brilliant youth,
   You once had fearless courage,
   You once had hope, had dreams, had love,

Right here
   Everything returns to the silence of reincarnation.

22

Hunger, viruses, war, rape, abuse,
   Extraordinary deaths have different faces,
   But the end is the same,
There is no order, no priority.

23

Foolish mankind,
    You will never understand
    True value,
The value of beauty,
The value of love,
The value of tolerance,
You use them,
And at the same time defiling them.

You chose power, oppression, slavery, lies, greed, fraud, hatred, and killing,
    Worship evil deeds as virtues,
    Even if Prometheus brought the holy fire
    Nor can it illuminate your eyes,
    Therefore, you will live in suffering from life to life,
    Only the fire of hell can wake you up,
    Could it be that the Creator has shaped you into
    Lower creatures driven by desires?

23

Never possible
In fraternity
Rise to the heights of beauty and goodness?

Hallelujah! hallelujah! hallelujah!

24

Evil spirits can always smell the rotten smell of human nature,
    Like hyenas stalking the dead bodies.

Soul
    Since when
    Became the base of Satan?
    Have we already given up our desires?
    Placed in the devil's feast?
    Can no longer bear the beautiful sunshine,
    But spread arms to embrace slaughter?

25

People, let us confess your sins together,
   Even the fire of hell cannot burn away your native evil,
Where the fingers stretch,
Desires, darkness and destruction lurk,
In the place where wish lives,
It must also be filled with the smell of evil spirits.

26

"I also devoted myself to discerning wisdom, arrogance and folly,
 I realize that this is also chasing the wind.
Because there is much wisdom, there is much sorrow;
He who increases knowledge increases sorrow." [1]

"You heard the saying:
 'Love your neighbor and hate your enemy.'
 But I tell you the truth,
 Love your enemies and pray for those who persecute you… If someone slaps you on your right cheek, let him slap you on the other cheek as well;
 If someone asks for your coat, let him take your outer garment too;
 If someone forces you to run one mile, go with him and run two miles." [2]

"You see the mountains and think they are all fixed, but in fact they all pass away like moving clouds."

"Saving one person is like saving all mankind."

"We have removed your veil, and now your eyes see clearly that I created all living things out of water. Don't they believe it?"

"Love your neighbor as yourself." [3]

"gate gate pāragate pārasaṃgate bodhi svāhā." [4]

"ong ā mī dē wǎ ā yī sī dé hòng shē." [5]

"Three hundred thousand times, the Buddha appeared in the unknown state without any preconditions.

Afterwards, he dedicated his life to making a wish to eliminate untimely death in this world.

There is a shortcut to the deep bliss of the next life, so we have the opportunity to practice it." [6]

[1]

"Old Testament·Ecclesiastes" Chapter 1

[2]

"New Testament·Gospel of Matthew" Chapter 7

[3]

"The Holy Quran"

[4]

Sanskrit "Heart Sutra"

English: "Jiedi Jiedi Polo Jiedi Monk Jiedi Bodhisattva Maha"

[5]

"Amitabha Buddha's Great Joy Heart Mantra"

[6]

"Shurangama Mantra"

27

Have you ever seen Sakyamuni walking barefoot in the wasteland of this world?
That once luxurious prince,
His mercy grew out from the suffering and hunger of the world;
Jesus is still weeping while suffering on the cross;
The Prophet Muhammad still meditates with the Koran in his hands;
Confucius, the sage who was based on benevolence,
Watching the world's bloody rivers of carnage alone.

28

Angels are wandering in the sky
    Looking down at the world with compassion,
    With love,
With pity,
With helplessness.

29

Come from the wind
    Return to wind;

From the water
    Return to water;

From the dust
    Return to dust;

From the air
    Return to air;

Everything is empty,
    Empty but not empty!

January 16, 2024, New York

On the Spirituality of the 21st Century Poetry

P oets are translators of human's soul.

The purpose of the existence of poetry is to transcend the limits of matter, as a person, that is, to transcend the limits of the body, so that thoughts and emotions appear as a pure spiritual existence. The actual appearance is peeled off layer by layer, and finally presents the essence of absolute life.

How can we transform the thoughts and emotions in our minds with the flows of consciousness into words that can be seen as real visions in the eyes of readers? In poetry, everything is driven by imagination, which must address the significance of the imagination to the poet and the unique strengths of poetry.

No other art forms can freely expand and deeply convey the inner world of human beings, the subtle states of thoughts and emotions, the changes and transformations between them as in poetry. Fortunately, poets are precisely the most imaginative human beings, and they should be the best persons to capture human emotions and sentiments. The poet has the ability to squint his soul to fly in the sky, to enter the earth, to experience the various possible states of spiritual existence; he can start from a simple word, idiom, sentence, object, endlessly associates that with images, finally cast them into extraordinary significant lines of poetry. We cannot imagine that a great poet does not have such qualities. So how does imagination develop in the creation of poetry?

We have two ways to imagine in the process of writing: the first way, is to, completely without control, let the imagination of the streams of consciousness naturally determine its directions, the poet only needs to do is to follow it, record its development trajectory, thus forming lines of sentences, this situation is usually carried out in the subconscious, can unearth the psychological level that is ignored in the daily life. The second way, is to, first, decide the directions to imagine, and then follow their development process. This method of writing is beneficial to the overall structure of the poem and helps the poet to complete a magnificent poetry.

As for how to cultivate imagination, many theorists of poetry have already discussed it. What I want to describe here is, how to make the imagination unfold in the strongest way to reproduce the reality of the spiritual world.

Imagination can be unfolded in all spaces. From the psychological level of analysis, the formation of sensory power is always achieved through contrast. Various contrasts, such as colors, shapes, sizes, light and shade, can always have a shocking effect on our psychology. In the case of poetry, when our imagination is between the smallest microscopic (such as particles) and the largest macro (such as the universe), the power of imagination, on the psychological level, is in maximized satisfaction, realized in the highest sense, that is to say, the formation of the greatest psychological power is produced among two or more extreme contrasts of different or similar things. The same contrast can be developed between the beauty and the ugliness of things, and get a similar effect, as the contrast weakens, the psychological influence is correspondingly reduced. We should understand that there are also some poets whose concern is not with the extraordinary spiritual shock expressed by poetry, but by another kind of soft, graceful feelings. Such a poet is always surrounded by a specific kind of sentiment, and whose life is written in such a state of mind, such as the American poet Emily Dickinson, which is another matter.

The imaginations of poetry may unfold in different ways: they can be parallel or overlapping, they can be small and large, they can be large and small, they can be flat, or they can be geometrically constructed. All these are not the same.

In the process of writing, the further expansion and extended description of imagination is extremely necessary and very meaningful. It can expand the connotation of the text and make it present an extraordinary quality. Among them, the image description of the thinking thread is a powerful complement to the image description of vision.

On the Spirituality of the 21st Century Poetry

Today, in the big explosion of knowledge and understanding, we have a new approach, concept and perspective to the material world. The difference between material and spirituality can only be a relative concept. We are getting closer and closer to the concept that the universe comes from The One and goes back to The One. In the creation of poetry, it is very necessary for poets to go further in the depth of expression of the material world as well as the spiritual world. On the one hand, we try our best to explore the various possibilities of the human spiritual world, the subtle differences between emotions and feelings. We must break through the framework of predecessors, limits from the traditional concepts, and explore the lexical and grammatical features more creatively to reveal contemporary humanistic spirit. Based on the rhythm of the soul, with the development of emotions, the lexical and syntactic methods would be changed. The format of the verse does not have to be rigid, so that the poetry can convey the characteristics of contemporary life. On the other hand, the expression of poetry in the material world should reflect the features of our times. The characteristics of this era reflect the current world in science, technology and information explosion, the state of the external world in which human beings are located, the phraseological references and vocabularies of science, technology, information, biology, artificial intelligence not only can not be ruled out, but also necessary. In the context of micro and macro, the differences, contrasts and blends between them are revealed, so that poetry has the rigidity of the material in the real world.

Excessive romantic feeling may be a poison for poetry, because it will make the poet lose the deep involvement as well as expression of human spirit, and indulge in emotions without being restrained. In poetry, as in life, it is harmful. It is easy to make poetry a catharsis of superficial personal emotions. As far as words are concerned, the passionate, imaginative, flamboyant descriptions mixing with simple narration of plain tiling in poetry will receive unexpected dramatic effects. The result is that the impressions of both are strengthened. Such a result makes poetry have a more profound connotation, but also increases the richness of poetry in the field of formal expression.

The segmentation of language is a very interesting topic. It appears in the most unexpected changes in the writing process of poetry, such as: length, jump, shortage, symbolization, meaning division, etc., challenging human sensory nerves, to make our feelings satisfied in affright. Because the language is in a state of segmentation, it does not convey complete information to us. It is precisely because of such an incomplete state that it leaves more psychological space to be understood and developed, and the ideological trajectory to be interpreted makes the poetry quality present a special meaning. Not all poetry lines need to be understood rationally. Some sentences are merely confiding to consciousness, and only need to stay in the senses of consciousness.

"Non-empirical writing" is another very interesting topic. Most poetry writers are only used to writing in a well known process. Very few truly outstanding poets have the kind of constantly changing and updating their writing style. The ability to always make your creative process in an unknown uncertainty, to seek breakthroughs and development. This uncertain situation makes the poet shudder and inspires his imagination and extraordinary inspiration.

The reverse usage of lexical meaning can also add intriguing and inspiring expressions to the connotation of poetry. In a context of common sense, readers have to quest their own thinking. At this time, all the vocabulary is active in the reader's mind, and the verse can achieve extraordinary results. The reversal of lexical meaning is not only a challenge to consciousness, but also a challenge to the usage of language itself.

In the creation of contemporary poetry, it is not necessary to stick to the limitations of the past poetry or poetic theories. The exploration and development of poetry is a must for the poet. Scenes in life, stories, historical events, or intuition, derived thoughts, dreams in the pure spirituality, all can be, one after the other, randomly unfolded in the same poem. It is this multilevel fusion that makes the expression of a poem, achieve broad and profound results.

Scenes in life, stories, historical events, under the ingenious arrangement of poets, become far-reaching images in poetry; intuition, derived thoughts, dreams are important ways to explore the inner spirituality of human beings, because not everything in poetry is in rational and logical ways, sometimes it could be irrational and illogical, perhaps it is this seemingly irrational and illogical, which constitutes a deeper level of rationality and logic in the inner spirituality, and more profoundly reveals the essence existence of human life.

Or more directly, everything we understand is not necessarily a correct understanding. The history in the development of human society is the history to constantly correct the existing knowledge, and the history to constantly re-recognize ourselves and the world. The poet's writing should face the future and leave a spiritual room to be explored.

The grandeur and profoundness of the poet's spiritual vision can be realized in two aspects: micro and macro. In the process of poetry touching these two aspects, the imagination can find the world where it can really play a role. Traveling in such a broad field of vision as well as the micro territory, must be a landscape full of surprises and shocks, not only for nature, the world, the existence of human life can also be a panoramic refraction and reflection.

The best poet should be the best representative of the spirit of his times. From the perspective of an individual, the poet reflects the nature of individuality, and reflects the spiritual condition of human beings throughout the age. The poet expresses both for himself and for an era. This individual's thoughts and emotions also reflect the universality of human nature; poets cannot belong only to oneself, but must belong to an era.

The "non-personal" theory of poetry proposed by Eliot opposes the romantic tendency of poetry to regard poetry as a personal tendency of self-feeling. "Poetry is not indulging feelings, but escaping feelings, not expressing individuality, but escaping individuality." He also said that "the feelings of art are non-personalized." From this, he argued that literary criticism and literary appreciation should shift interest from the poet to the poem itself. Even from the scientific point of view, such a proposal is impossible to achieve, poets do not have the expression without individual emotional intervention. Moreover, the characteristics of individual emotion are the key to the formation of excellent poetry. Even Eliot's own poetry, what attracted us most was his personal traits rather than the commonality he advocated.

The poetry of an era is only a slice in history. Because of this, the poet should have a sense of history and write in the depth of history, so that poetry can convey a richer humanistic connotation, making poetry a veritable humanistic ark, a humanitarian bridge between past and future, not only has the inheritance of the spirit of human history, but also the prospect of the future of humanity.

In the 21st century, with the process of globalization, due to the general degeneration of human nature, selfishness, greed, prejudice, and the game of geographical interests worldwide, it has rapidly infected the entire human race, resulting in the general loss of the human spirit. We have no idealistic feelings in the humanistic spirit that once inspired humanity. In such a realistic context, the poems of the 21st century, as the bearing of human pure soul, to express humanistic care and express humanistic ideals, is extremely important.

Finally, it should be pointed out that any theory about poetry creation cannot replace the deep experience of life itself. This kind of experience needs long-term persistence and constant renewal, and cannot be accomplished overnight. This is why many well learned people, because of the lack of profound experience and sentiment about life itself, it is the reason why

MEDITATION AT THE FOOT OF THE HIMALAYAS

they never have created great poems ; it is why some poets have created excellent poems, and later, because of the lack of real feelings about life, can't write a good poem anymore.

November 30, 2008, New York

POSTSCRIPT

For decades, many cherished people and things in life have left me. Those nameless touches, sorrows and tears of life have made me realize the meaning of this life. Although they were shaking apart, silent in the tunnel of time. With the infiltration of the years, they have developed unconsciously, blending with the emotions of reality and inspiring new and strong emotions. In this uneasy and complicated state of mind, I felt the need to record these feelings.

A person could have many lives, every morning woke up from dreams, I regarded myself have regained a new life, and because of this, filled with appreciation to people and this world, however, a person could only have one spiritual home that deeply rooted in the soul, defined himself who he was, awaking him at midnight, calling him to return. This was the reason I kept writing poetry.

MEDITATION AT THE FOOT OF THE HIMALAYAS

Only in the poetry lines did I find the true hometown of my soul.

So as they were taken down.

About the Author

Shutao Liao, born on 25th August 1963, Zigong, Sichuan, China. He received Raffaello Sanzio Master Award, Shakespeare Award and Nelson Mandela Human Value Award in 2014, Honorary Master Member of Italian Cultural Association 2014, Honorary Master Member of Academy of Visual Art "Italia In Arte Nel Mondo" Cultural Association 2016. He is a world acclaimed artist, writer, poet and humanist.

His recent study was focused on the decay of humanity.

You can connect with me on:
🌐 https://liaoshutao.blogspot.com

Milton Keynes UK
Ingram Content Group UK Ltd.
UKHW041042181024
449742UK00021B/34